Maya Angelou Finds Her Voice

Maya Angelou Finds Her Voice

By CONNIE & PETER ROOP
Illustrated by NOA DENMON

ALADDIN
New York   London   Toronto   Sydney   New Delhi

Maya Angelou loved words.

She whispered, "*caterpillar green*" just to paint the color in her mind.

Her tongue played with "PANDEMO

She barked, "STARK" just to hear its hardness.

NIUM just to enjoy its rhythm.

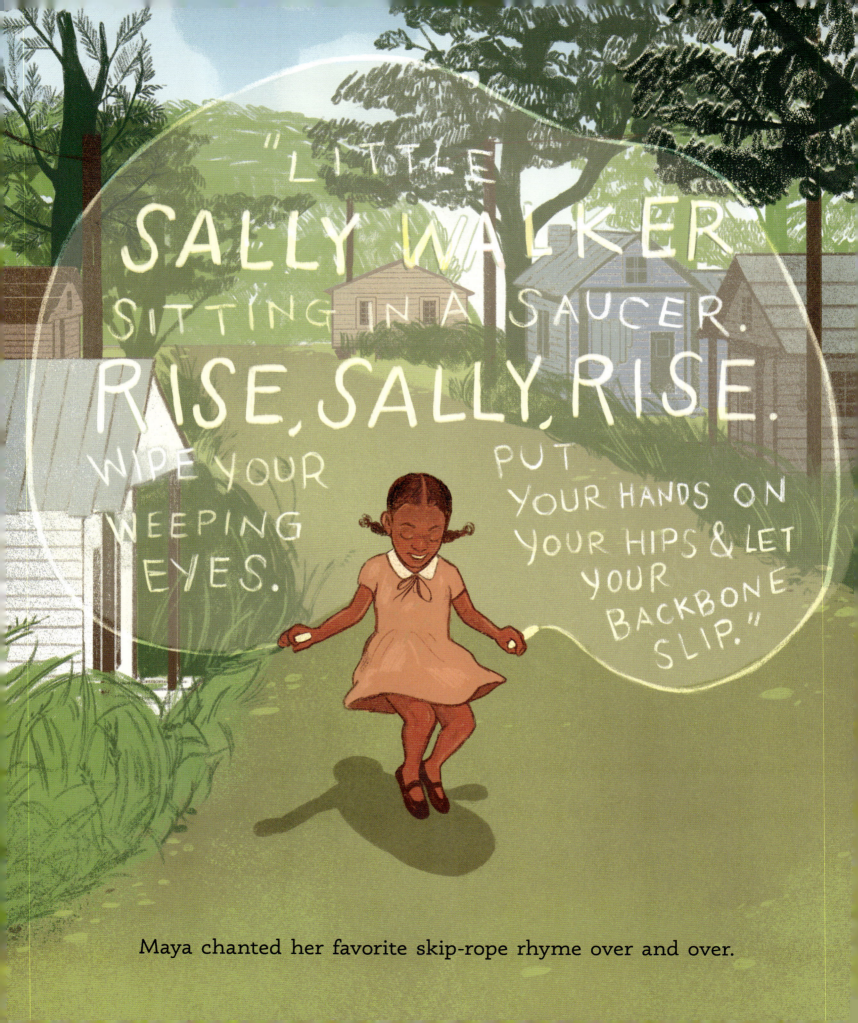

Maya chanted her favorite skip-rope rhyme over and over.

She enjoyed singing the "Black National Anthem."

And the poetry of Paul Laurence Dunbar spoke directly to her.

I know what the caged bird feels, alas!
When the sun is bright on the upland slopes;
When the wind stirs soft through the
 springing grass,
And the river flows like a stream of glass.

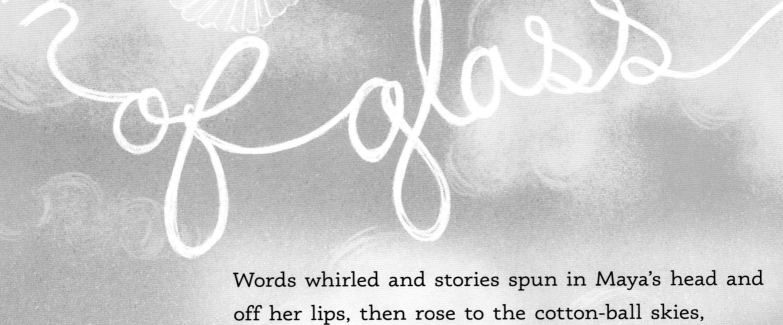

Words whirled and stories spun in Maya's head and off her lips, then rose to the cotton-ball skies,

helping her escape the troubled, segregated world . . . and soothing her soul.

Until, one day, eight-year-old Maya stopped talking.

She had been attacked.

And even though that person had caused her
painful trauma, Maya believed her confession—
her words—were responsible for his death.

She would not speak—
not to Momma, her wise grandmother,
not to her gentle uncle Willie,
not to her loud teacher,
not to her proud preacher.

Maya decided to speak *only* to her older brother Bailey. Her love for him was so strong, Maya was sure her words could *never* hurt him.

It was Bailey who had changed her name of Marguerite to Maya.

For years Maya did not speak.
But she read.
Voraciously.

And she listened:
to the *clickety-clack*,
the *screechity-scr-e-e-e-e-ch*,
the *chitter-chatter*,
and the *tee-hee-hee*s.

Maya's refusal to talk angered and frustrated those closest to her.

Yet it also worried them. But then . . .

One afternoon Mrs. Beulah Flowers entered Momma's store and smiled directly at Maya.

"Good day, Mrs. Henderson," Mrs. Flowers said to Momma, her voice rippling like a breeze.

Momma replied, "How are you today, Sister Flowers?"

As Mrs. Flowers chatted with Momma, Maya soaked in her words. She admired the way Mrs. Flowers spoke, the way she carried herself, the way she appeared to be a character stepping out of a book.

All these things made Maya proud of Mrs. Flowers.

Mrs. Flowers told Momma her order, and after Momma plucked each item from the shelves, Maya placed them in a grocery bag.

"Sister Flowers," Momma said, "Bailey will bring your groceries to your house."

"Thank you, Mrs. Henderson," said Mrs. Flowers. "I'd prefer to have Marguerite carry my groceries. I've been wanting to speak to her."

Mrs. Flowers used Maya's given name, Marguerite, not the nickname Bailey had given her.

As they walked on the narrow, rocky path winding uphill to her house, Mrs. Flowers said to Maya, "Your teacher tells me that you are a good student. *But* only on your written work. She said that you refuse to talk in class."

Maya was silent.

"Walk beside me," Mrs. Flowers urged. "Marguerite," she said. "No one is going to make you talk if you don't want to. Possibly no one can. But remember, language is our way of communicating with other people. Language separates us from animals."

At her house Mrs. Flowers served Maya a plate of her homemade tea cakes.

Mrs. Flowers then gave her the first of what Maya later called "my lessons in living."

Mrs. Flowers said, "I am going to loan you some books, Marguerite. I want you to read them out loud, not silently. And I'll accept no excuse if you return a book to me that has been damaged."

Mrs. Flowers selected her favorite book, a well-worn copy of *A Tale of Two Cities*, and began reading.

"It was the best of times,
it was the worst of times,
it was the age of wisdom,
it was the age of foolishness..."

Mrs. Flowers's melodic voice slid in and curved down and through and over the words.

Her syllables drifted upward, dancing in the air.

IT WAS THE BEST

In that moment Maya felt like all the light in the world had enveloped her in the poetry of Mrs. Flowers reciting the words of Charles Dickens.

"Did you like that?" asked Mrs. Flowers.

"Yes, ma'am!"
Maya exclaimed.

Maya had spoken!

She felt that speaking was the least she could do for Mrs. Flowers.

And Maya understood that speaking was important for her, too.

"Marguerite, there is one more thing," Mrs. Flowers said. "Please take this book of poems and memorize one for me. The next time you pay me a visit, I want you to recite it."

Clutching the books and a bag of tea cakes close to her, Maya ran back to the store and to her family.

In that afternoon Mrs. Flowers had given Maya the key to unlock her voice, now finally free to rise up and inspire the world.

And she did.

AUTHORS' NOTE

MAYA ANGELOU'S BOOK *I Know Why the Caged Bird Sings* was our primary source. In this autobiography, Maya shares the traumatic assault that preceded her decision to be mute. Mrs. Flowers's love of words and books inspired Maya to once again use her remarkable voice, a voice that turned experiences of pain into a life of purpose, a voice that impacted our world.

We conducted research on two visits to Maya's hometown of Stamps, Arkansas, where Maya's story takes place.

We located the site of the store where Maya began carrying Mrs. Flowers's groceries.

We walked in Maya's footsteps where she followed Mrs. Flowers to her home.

We saw Maya's segregated school, the Lafayette County Training School, which Maya attended from grades one through eight. There she sang what was called at that time the "Negro National Anthem."

Today it is known as the "Black National Anthem."

Along the shores of Lake June in Stamps (where Maya often read alone), we shared Maya's words about her life-changing talk with Mrs. Flowers. Today Maya Angelou City Park on Lake June honors Maya.

We also visited Wake Forest University in Winston-Salem, North Carolina. There we read many of Maya's literary papers, which are archived in the Wake Forest library. Here we had the opportunity and pleasure to talk with people who knew Maya Angelou.

The Schomburg Center for Research in Black Culture in Harlem also proved invaluable. Here we read more of Maya's own handwritten words and manuscripts.

We would like to thank the mayor and the staff of the city hall of Stamps, Arkansas, for directing us to Maya Angelou sites.

Profound thanks to the dedicated staff of the archives at Wake Forest University and at the Schomburg Center, for welcoming us and expertly sharing Maya Angelou's manuscripts and papers.

Special thanks to Karen Nagel for having faith in our manuscript and to Laura Lyn DiSiena for selecting Noa Denmon to illustrate our story.

Last, but not least, a big shout-out to Susan Cohen, agent and friend.

Thank you, Susan, for being such a fan and supporter over all these years. Best of luck in your "retirement." We already miss you!

For Abbie and her friend Maya, who both love words and books
—C. R. & P. R.

To Tyler and Bruce for being by my side every step of the way
—N. D.

ALADDIN • An imprint of Simon & Schuster Children's Publishing Division • 1230 Avenue of the Americas, New York, New York 10020 • First Aladdin hardcover edition January 2025 • Text copyright © 2025 by Peter Roop and Connie Roop • Illustrations copyright © 2025 by Noa Denmon • All rights reserved, including the right of reproduction in whole or in part in any form. • ALADDIN and related logo are registered trademarks of Simon & Schuster, LLC. • For information about special discounts for bulk purchases, please contact Simon & Schuster Special Sales at 1-866-506-1949 or business@simonandschuster.com. • The Simon & Schuster Speakers Bureau can bring authors to your live event. For more information or to book an event contact the Simon & Schuster Speakers Bureau at 1-866-248-3049 or visit our website at www.simonspeakers.com. • Book designed by Laura Lyn DiSiena • The illustrations for this book were rendered digitally. • The text of this book was set in Phoreus Cherokee. • Manufactured in China 0924 SCP • 2 4 6 8 10 9 7 5 3 1 • Library of Congress Control Number 2024933930 • ISBN 9781481449267 • ISBN 9781481449281 (ebook)